Illustrations by
Marisa Vestita

THE MOST BEAUTIFUL FABLES OF
AESOP, PHAEDRUS AND
LA FONTAINE

Introduction

This magnificently illustrated volume includes 36 of the most famous and fanciful fables compiled by the three great fabulists of classic literature : Aesop, Phaedrus and La Fontaine. The literary genre of the fable, the origin of which is lost in the mists of time, features brief compositions, in prose or verse, with anthropomorphized animals as the main character. Their adventures – amusing or ironic, irreverent or simply bizarre – always have an underlying moral lesson, an ethical or behavioral maxim that aims at being universal in scope. Aesop, the first author to figure in this collection for chronological reasons (the Greek slave, who lived in the 6th century B.C., left us around 400 fables), has become a model for the literary genre as a whole, inspiring a slew of other authors who made a foray into this type of composition. Though centuries have passed, Aesop's short, simple fables – with their focus on completely human behaviors and habits that no reader can fail to identify with – haven't lost their ability to interest and amuse readers young and old.

The second part of this volume is devoted to another slave; an exponent, this time, of Latin literature (Phaedrus wrote around 100 fables in the 1st century A.D.). The animals depicted in Phaedrus's short tales are clever or terribly foolish, proud or vain, honest or liars… but always irresistibly entertaining and capable of turning each and every composition into a small masterpiece of irony and lightness. And the verses composed in the 17th century by French poet Jean de La Fontaine, whose fables conclude this volume, certainly drew on the works by the two ancient fabulists. Featuring a refined yet simple style, his tales have greatly influenced European literature, perhaps by virtue of their veiled, ironic social criticism. The fables presented in the following pages, readapted for a modern public, make use of a simple and easily accessible language to win over their youngest readers, who will enjoy reading about these amusing animals… smiling as they learn several important truths about human nature along the way.

Table of Contents

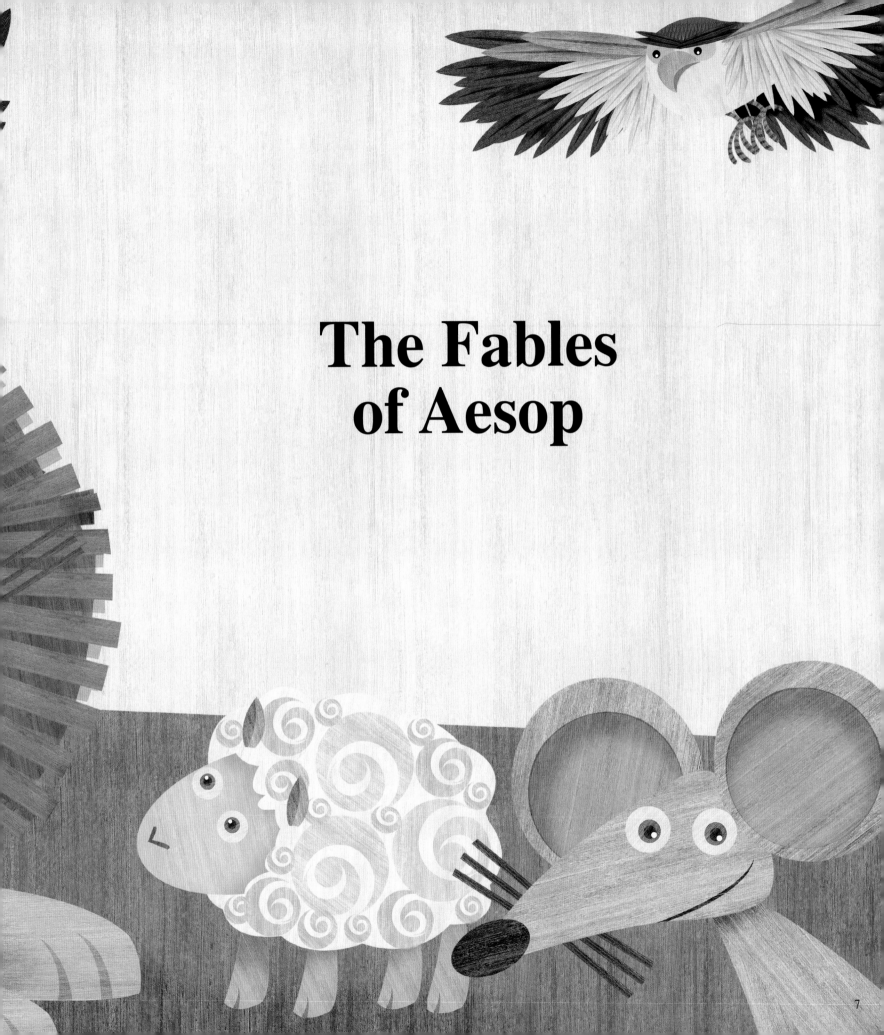

The Fables
of Aesop

The Gnat and the Lion

There once was a tiny gnat,
both cocky and clever.
Tired of playing with his
usual friends, one day
he decided to challenge
the King of the Forest.
So he came before the Lion

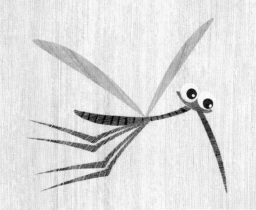

and bowed

respectfully to him.

The great King,

busy

enjoying

one

of his naps

along

the riverbank,

glanced

distractedly

at the insect.

"Oh!
Good morning,"
he answered with
a mighty yawn.
The Gnat said:
"Sire, I'm here
to challenge you!"
Suddenly interested,
the Lion woke up
and actually listened.

"You think you're the
strongest among animals,"
added the insect.
"Yet I'm sure
I could conquer you
in a duel!"

Amused, the Lion answered: "Well, then, if you're so sure... let's give it a try!"

The clearing filled in no time with animals of all sorts, eager to witness the duel which promptly begun. Flying over to the Lion, the insect settled on his opponent's wide nose and began stinging him sharply. The poor, startled Lion struck at the Gnat with his paws but,

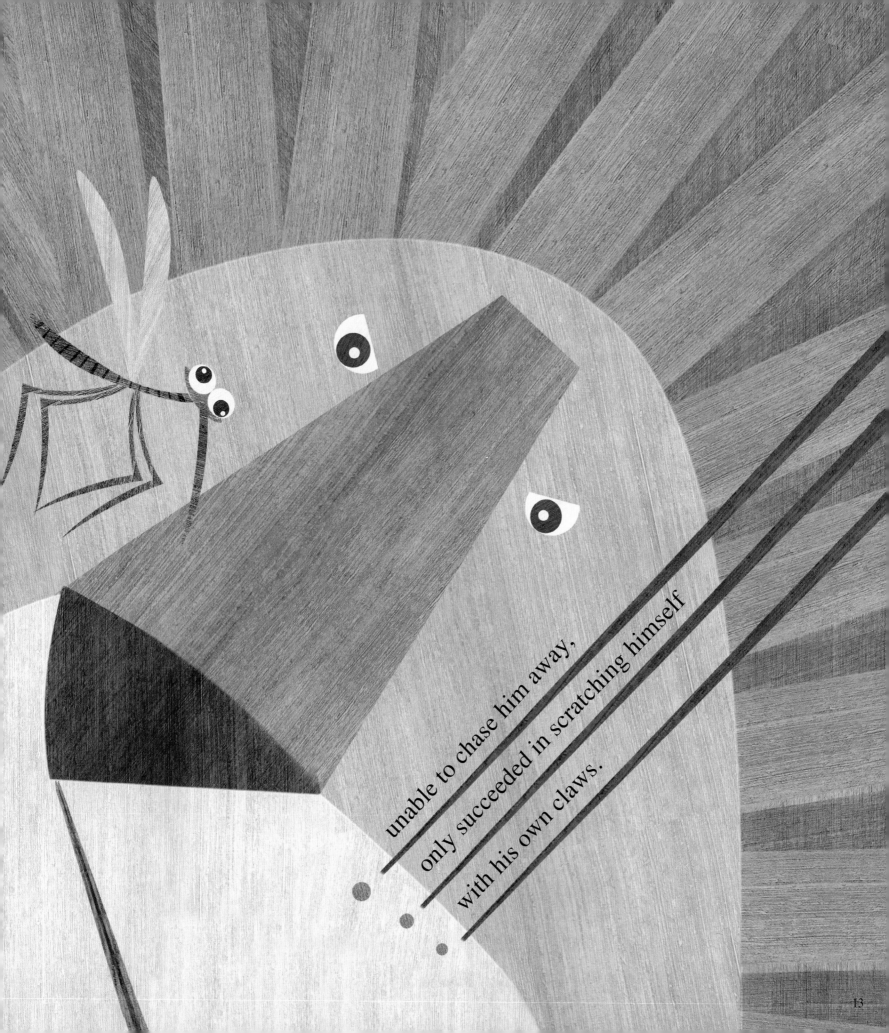

unable to chase him away,
only succeeded in scratching himself
with his own claws.

13

Worn out,
the King of the Forest
threw himself
on the ground in defeat
and the tiny Gnat
was proclaimed the winner
by all the beasts present.
As it flew away in triumph,
however,
the insect failed to notice
a spider web spun
between two branches

and became entangled in its meshes.

Trapped in that treacherous web,
and realizing the danger he was in,
the Gnat burst into tears.

Fortunately, the Lion – who had witnessed
the whole scene – brushed the web away,
saving the tiny insect's life.
"You're free, my dear friend," he said.
"And don't forget – there is always someone
stronger than you! That's something I learned from you…"
And so, from that day forth, the Gnat learned
to be less cocky.

The Fox and the Crow

A Crow, having stolen a piece of meat,
perched upon a tree branch.
Seeing this, the Fox instantly longed
to eat the succulent bite himself.
So the wily animal began to flatter the bird
from the foot of the tree,
admiring her perfect shape and glossy feathers,
and adding that no one was more deserving
of being hailed as Queen of Birds…
if only her voice matched her beauty.

And so, anxious to show off her voice,
the Crow let out a loud caw…
dropping the meat straight
into the Fox's mouth!
"My dear Crow," he added,
"you would surely
be hailed as Queen…
if only you had enough wits!"

The Kite and the Snake

A young Snake was slithering from rock to rock
without a care in the world,
enjoying the spring sunlight
on his back.
The air was warm and scented with flowers,
and the lovely weather made
all the animals feel happier.
The Snake was moving slowly
through the meadow when
a frightening shadow suddenly appeared
along his path.

The animal looked up worriedly to see
what had cast the dark shadow;
and that's when he saw a fearsome Kite
swooping down on him!

The poor Snake didn't stand a chance
as the bird of prey caught him in its beak and flew away
with him at the speed of light,
ignoring his cries.

"Let me go!"

Begged the unfortunate animal.
"I haven't done anything to you!"
But the Kite just ignored him.

At that point, the young Snake
twisted around and, in a clever move,
managed to bite his enemy.
Struck by its prey's venom, the bird was forced
to open its beak, thus freeing
the Snake who fell to the ground, unharmed.
The Kite, on the other hand, its sight blurred
and weakened by the venomous bite,
plummeted to the ground
and rolled over on some rocks, seriously hurting itself.

While the bird was still dazed, the young Snake slithered over to it and said:

"Serves you right!

You made me hurt you even though I didn't want to,
and now you're paying the price!"
The Kite couldn't fly for two days and,
from that moment on, always kept a
safe distance from all snakes!

The Boy Who Cried Wolf

A shepherd boy, bored with watching
his flock of sheep every day, decided to
play a prank on the other villagers.

Armed with pitchforks and clubs, the villagers all rushed to his aid,
but when they arrived at the meadow, there were no wolves to be seen.
All they found was the shepherd boy,
doubled over with laughter.
"It was only a prank… and you fell for it!"

The same thing happened a few days later, and the villagers,
rushing to the shepherd boy's aid, soon realized
that he had fooled them once again.

One day, though, a pack of wolves
arrived suddenly to attack his flock; the shepherd boy
began calling out for the villagers who,
sure he was trying to fool them again,
refused to come. And so the wolves, undisturbed,
killed off all his lambs and sheep.

The Crow and the Pitcher

A thirsty Crow found a pitcher
that had once been full,
but when he tried to drink from it,
discovered that there was only a little water
left on the bottom.

No matter how hard he tried to drink,
his long beak kept getting
stuck in the pitcher!
Nearly desperate by now,
the Crow was struck by an idea:
picking up a pebble, he
dropped it into the pitcher.

He picked up another, and dropped it into the pitcher again,

and then a third pebble,

and a fourth.

Then, picking up a fifth pebble,

he did the same.

39

As he kept dropping pebbles
into the pitcher, one by one,
the water slowly began to rise to the top,
and the Crow was finally able to drink.

The Fox and the Grapes

One day, a famished Fox saw
some clusters of grapes hanging upon a vine
and wanted to taste them.
Unable to reach them, however,
she turned away, saying to herself:
"Those grapes were sour, anyway."

The Tortoise and the Hare

"No one can run as fast as I," the Hare boasted
to the other animals in the forest. "I challenge anyone
to beat me in a race!"
Slow and steady as ever, the Tortoise said:
"I accept your challenge."

"That's a good one!"
exclaimed the Hare
as he burst out laughing.

"Don't brag until you've won…"
replied the Tortoise.
"Do you want to run this race or not?"
And so the course was chosen
and the opponents
were off!

The Hare set off
like a shot:
so far ahead
he was almost
out of sight. Then he slowed down
and, to show his disdain for the Tortoise,
stretched out by the road
to take a nap.
Meanwhile, the Tortoise struggled along,
with her slow and steady pace, but when
the Hare woke up, he saw his rival almost
at the finish line.

So he started running as fast as he could,
but it was too late to overcome his opponent.
With a smile, the Tortoise said:

"Slow and steady wins the race."

The Fox with the Swollen Belly

Winter was approaching.
The bare trees no longer offered shelter,
and the little animals had gotten ready
to face the cold. A very hungry young Fox,
on the other hand, was wandering through
the woods in search of food.
He hadn't eaten in several days, as the
animals he usually hunted were by now
holed up in the toasty warmth of their
burrows with the food they had stored up
over the summer, and were impossible
to drive out.
So the poor animal wandered dejectedly to
and fro, reflecting that hunger was
the worst possible companion.

All of a sudden, a delicious smell tickled his nostrils. Following the smell, the Fox spotted an enormous hunk of roast meat placed in the hollow of an oak – it looked as though some shepherds had forgotten their lunch!

Though it was a tight squeeze, the Fox managed to
push his way into the hole, where he gobbled up
the delicious meat. A few minutes later, with
his belly as full as could be, he decided it
was time to go back to the forest.

But as soon as he tried to
leave the way he came…
he realized that he couldn't get out!
He had eaten so much
that his belly was swollen!
Scared out of his mind, he tried to
squeeze back out, but only
succeeded in getting stuck in the hole!

The unlucky animal began to groan and yell.
Another Fox, passing by,
heard his cries and stopped to see what had
happened. "It's no use complaining. All you
had to do was wait patiently inside that hole
until your belly got smaller.
Instead, you were greedy and stuffed
yourself, and now you'll have to wait until
you've digested all
that food."

And so the poor Fox stayed stuck in the hole for the entire day,
lamenting the toasty warmth he would have enjoyed
if he had just waited patiently inside the hollow oak.

The Ant and the Grasshopper

On a cold winter's day,
as the Ants left
the anthill to dry their
rain-soaked seeds,
they met
a starving Grasshopper
who begged them for some food.

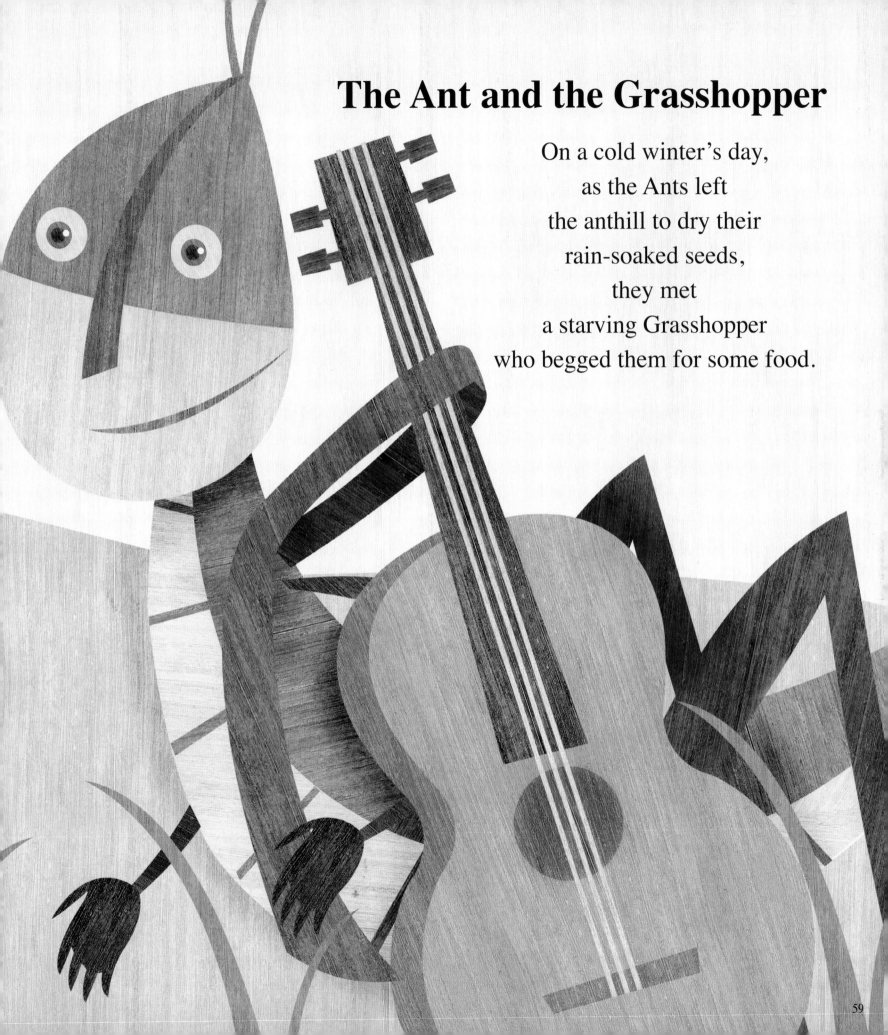

"Why didn't you store up any food
during the summer, like us?" asked the Ants.
"I was certainly not idle," replied the Grasshopper.
"I spent the summer days singing."
"Well, then," the Ants retorted with a derisive laugh,
"If you sang all summer long, you can dance
all winter!"

The Lion and the Mouse

A Lion lay asleep under a tree as some country Mice were chasing each other along one of the branches.
All of a sudden, one of the Mice tripped and accidentally fell on the sleeping King of the Forest! Furious at this brusque awakening, the King pounced on the little Mouse, about to kill her.

She begged him to forgive her,
promising lifelong devotion
in exchange.
Amused, the Lion decided
to let her go.
A few days later, he was caught
in a snare set by some hunters,
and found himself unable to move
or escape. The Mouse, hearing his
angry roars, rushed to his aid, nimbly
gnawing the rope with her teeth.

After setting the Lion free, she said:

"You once laughed at me

because you didn't think

I could ever return the favor.

Now you know
that even
the smallest creatures
can help
the greatest ones!"

The Wild Donkey and the Tame Donkey

There once was a Wild Donkey
who spent his days wandering freely
from field to field,
eating everything he found.
One day, during his usual stroll,
he spotted a fellow Donkey,
healthy and strong, grazing a meadow
surrounded by a high wood fence.
As he watched his tame cousin,
the Donkey thought:
"What a great life!
Peaceful, carefree and
all the food you could want."

And, indeed, the other Donkey seemed to lead a charmed life:
he had two hearty meals a day, a warm stable to sleep in
and a magnificent meadow where he could graze
to his heart's content. The Wild Donkey, on the other hand,
had to make do with the measly shrubs he could find
by the side of the road, since all the grassy meadows
were fenced off.

Sometimes the poor little Donkey would rest his muzzle
on the fence, staring enviously at his fellow creature.
Then one day, as he was strolling along as usual, the Donkey met
an animal so laden with wood, sacks of grain and more that
he almost didn't recognize him.

Only when the animal raised its head to kick at its master,
in return for a violent whiplash, did our Donkey realize
it was the Tame Donkey that he used to envy so much!
"My dear friend," he said, walking up to the other,
"I'd never trade lives with you, not at this price!
I may not eat as richly as you, but I'm as light
and free as a bird…
and I certainly don't take
orders from anyone!"

And from that day on, the Wild Donkey never envied
his fellow creature again.

The Shepherd
and the Wolf

A Wolf got into the habit
    of prowling around a flock of sheep,
    without, however, doing them
    any harm.
        Believing him to be an enemy,
        the suspicious Shepherd kept
        a watchful eye
        on him at first,
        but the Wolf hung
        around stubbornly,
        never threatening
        the flock in the least.

Little by little, the Shepherd
came to believe he was an excellent guardian,
rather than a threat…
even going so far as to leave his sheep
in the Wolf's care when he went to town.

But the Wolf, seizing his chance,
rushed at the sheep,
swallowing most of them up whole.
When the Shepherd came back and saw what had happened,
he exclaimed:
"It serves me right for being so foolish
as to leave my flock in a Wolf's care!"

The Fables
of Phaedrus

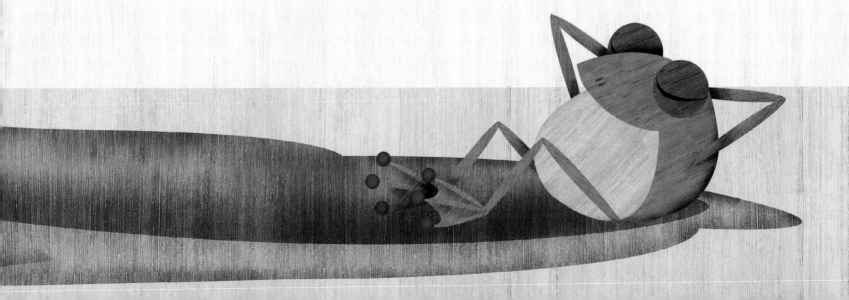

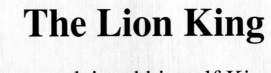

The Lion King

When the Lion proclaimed himself King of the Forest,
he gave up his old habits
and, making do with little food,
began to dispense justice with great fairness.
As time went on, however,
this new lifestyle began to weigh on him.

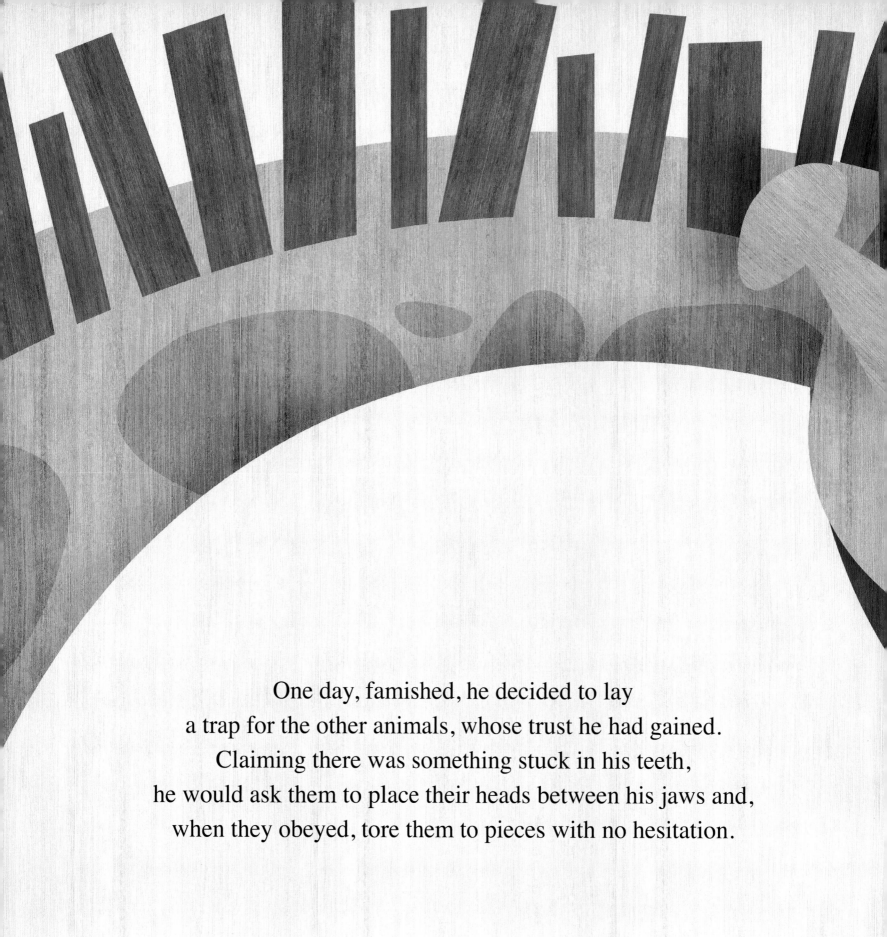

One day, famished, he decided to lay
a trap for the other animals, whose trust he had gained.
Claiming there was something stuck in his teeth,
he would ask them to place their heads between his jaws and,
when they obeyed, tore them to pieces with no hesitation.

When the Monkey's turn finally came,
he cleverly obeyed from afar, cleaning
the Lion's teeth by means of a long stick.
Frustrated, the Lion came up
with a new plan to trick him.

Pretending to be sick, here's
what he told the doctors busy
discussing the right medicine to prescribe:

"The only thing that can cure me is Monkey stew."

No sooner had the Lion spoken, than the doctors grabbed
the Monkey, sacrificing him for the good of their King.
And this time, no amount of cleverness
was enough to save his life!

The Dog and the Wolf

A scrawny, half-starved Wolf
chanced to meet a
plump, well-fed Dog.

"Tell me," he said,
"Where do you find all your food?
Though much stronger than you,
I'm dying of hunger."

The Dog replied:
"You'd soon find yourself
in the same condition
if you were willing
to serve my master
as I do: by guarding the door
and protecting his house
from thieves at night".

"I rather like the idea.

At the moment
I have to endure
rain and snow;
it would be so much
easier to have
a roof over my head
and eat as much
as I want
without doing
anything!"

"Come with me, then!"
urged the Dog.

But the Wolf soon
noticed the collar mark
on the Dog's neck.
"What happened to you, my friend?"
"Nothing much; they keep me tied up
by day, so I'll sleep when it's light out,
and stay awake at night.
They let me loose
at dusk, and I get to work
after my dinner.
And so my belly fills
with no effort on my part."

"And tell me – are you free
to wander about,
if you wish to?"
"Of course not," said the Dog.

"Then enjoy the meals
you boast of, friend Dog.
I wouldn't be a king,
if it meant not being free!"

103

The Fox
and the Ram

A Fox couldn't
get out of the deep well
into which he had carelessly fallen.
Along came a thirsty Ram, who
asked him if the water was plentiful
and sweet.

As sly as ever, the Fox replied:
"Climb down into the well, my friend;
I've never drunk fresher water!"

And the great bearded one jumped
in without a second thought.
The Fox swiftly climbed
those long horns and made his escape,
leaving the Ram on the bottom
of the well, with no way out.

The Stag at the Stream

A Stag, having drunk his fill,
stood gazing at his reflection
in the stream.
He looked upon his branching horns
with pride, but found fault
with the extreme
thinness of his legs.
Suddenly frightened by the voices
of the Huntsmen,
he took flight over the fields,
running swiftly towards the woods
to escape the dogs.

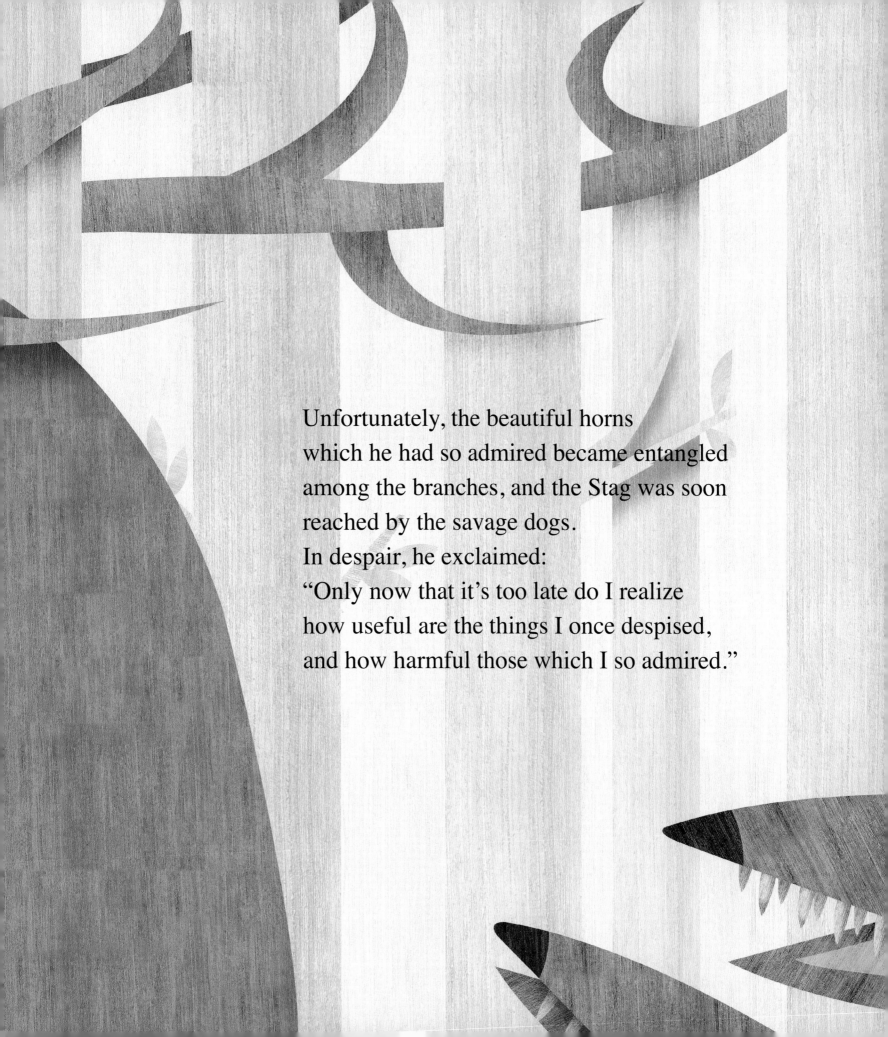

Unfortunately, the beautiful horns
which he had so admired became entangled
among the branches, and the Stag was soon
reached by the savage dogs.
In despair, he exclaimed:
"Only now that it's too late do I realize
how useful are the things I once despised,
and how harmful those which I so admired."

Dogs and Wolves Reconcile

Said the Wolves to the Dogs: "We're so similar,
yet why don't we get along?
Look at us: the only difference
lies in our disposition.
We roam freely, while you
are servants to Men,
and must guard their sheep.
Furthermore, they never throw
you more than a bone from their feasts.

It's time for a change:
have faith in us and
hand over all the sheep.
We promise to share them with you."

Sadly, the Dogs listened to the Wolves,
letting them into the pen.

And so the ravenous, dishonest Wolves
tore the gullible Dogs to pieces
before swallowing up all the sheep.

The Frogs Who Desired a King

Tired of living with no one to rule over them,
the Frogs sent a messenger to Jupiter,
begging him to give them a king.
And the god answered their prayers
by throwing a small log into their pond.

At first, terrified by the splash, the frogs dove into the water,
seeking shelter at the bottom of the pond.
After a while, seeing how the piece of wood never moved,
they rose back to the surface and slowly began to despise
that silent king, to the point where they would jump
or even sit on it.

Finally, embarrassed by such a ruler,
they returned to Jupiter
to ask for another one.
This time, though, Jupiter lost
his patience and sent them a water snake,
which ate up all the frogs in no time!

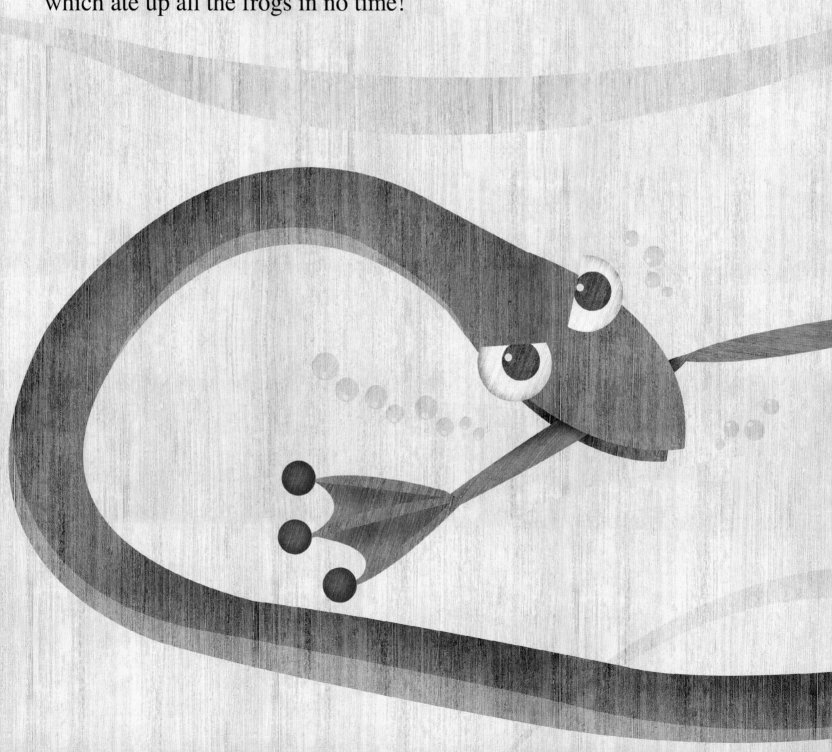

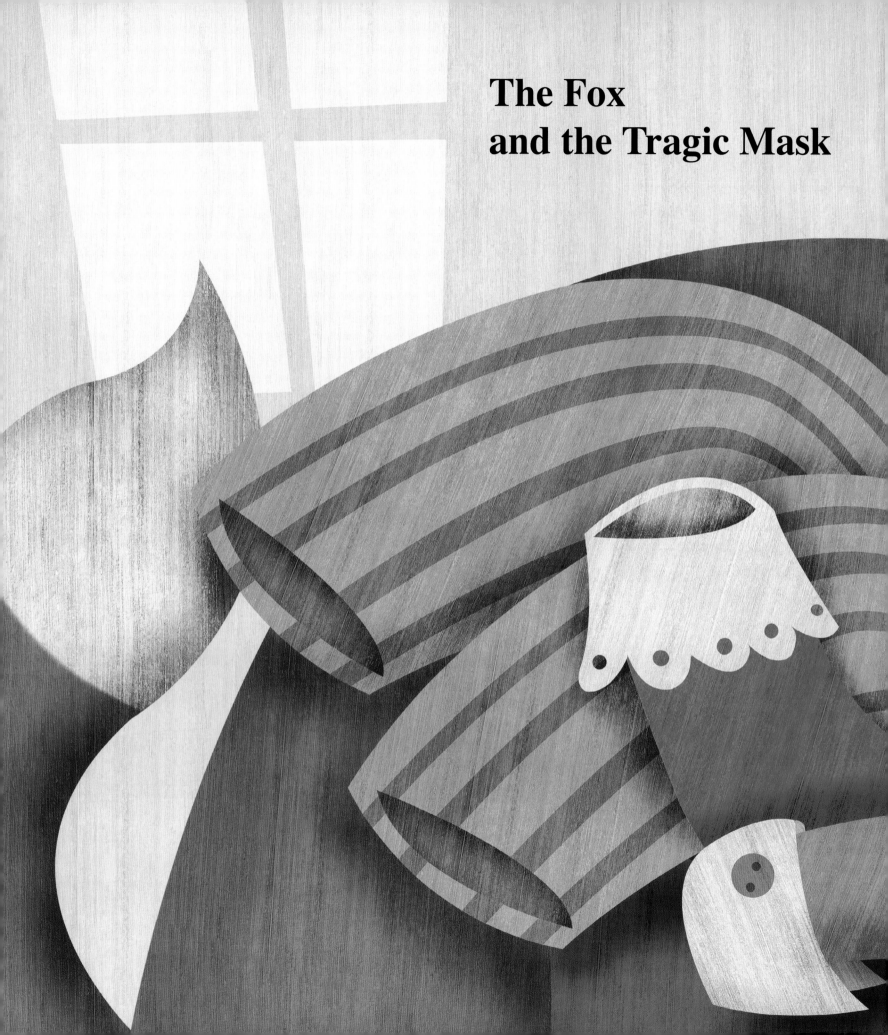

The Fox
and the Tragic Mask

One day, a Fox snuck into an Actor's home and came across an exceptionally well-made theater mask as he was rummaging through a trunkful of costumes.

Curious, he picked it up in his paws and said:

"Though you're a magnificent head,

you have no brains!"

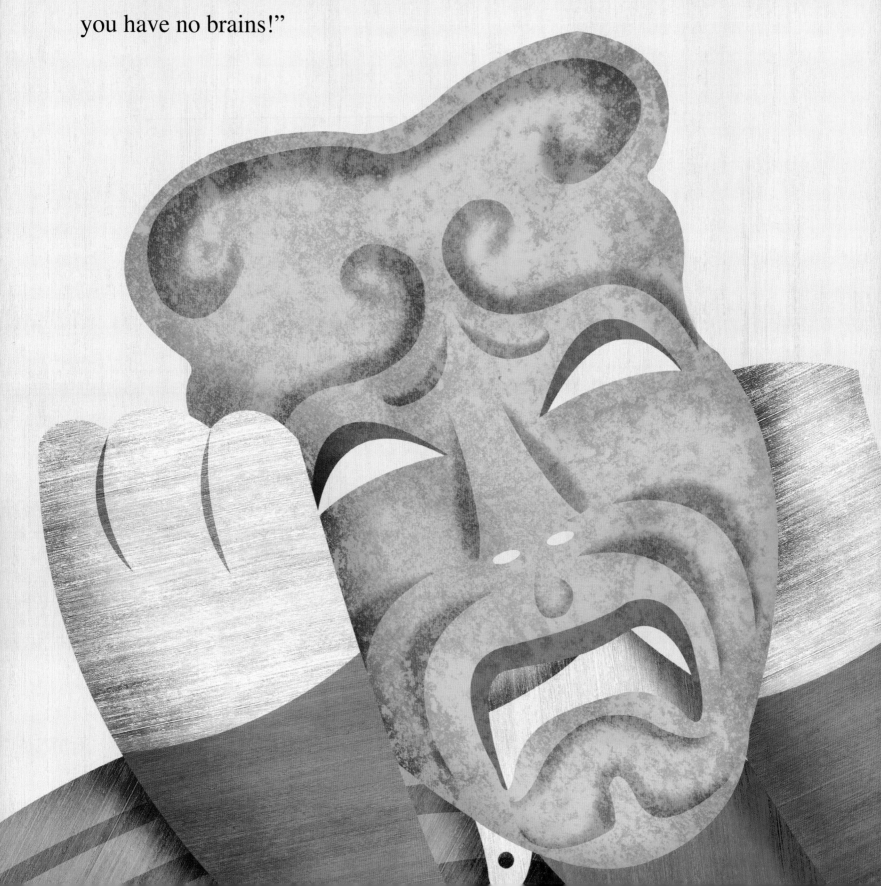

129

The Wolf and the Crane

One day, eating greedily, the Wolf
accidentally swallowed a bone
which got stuck in his throat.
Overcome with pain, he tried
to convince the other animals to help him,
meekly promising rewards and favors in return.

Lured by his promises, the Crane was finally
prevailed on to lower her long beak into the
Wolf's fearsome jaws, freeing him from the
irritating bone.

But when she demanded the promised reward,
the Wolf replied:

"How ungrateful!
After removing your head
from my mouth in complete safety,
what more could you possible wish for?"

The Bees
and Drones
with the Wasp
as Judge

After a swarm of Bees
had labored to build a beehive
high up in a tree,
some lazy Drones claimed
it as their own.

The matter was taken to court, with a Wasp sitting as judge. Well-acquainted with both parties, the Wasp decided that they should each build a new beehive:

it was the only way to find out
who the real owner of the honey was.
Ever lazy, the Drones refused to take on the challenge,
leaving the Wasp to pronounce his verdict:

"It is clear to us all
that the Bees built
the first beehive,
and to them I
hereby return it!"

The Frogs Alarmed by the Bullfight

A Frog, watching the Bulls fighting
from the safety of her pond, exclaimed:

"Alas! A tragedy is about to befall us!"

Another Frog asked why she said such a thing,
since the Bulls lived so far away.
The wise Frog replied:
"Their home may be far away,
but whoever is banished from the herd
will seek refuge in our pond,
crushing us under his hard hooves.

That's why their battles
concern us!"

The Wolf and the Fox
with the Monkey as Judge

The Wolf accused the Fox of theft,
while he claimed to be innocent,
so the Monkey sat as judge between them.

After they each told
their side of the story,
the Monkey ruled thus:

"You're both liars! You,"
he said to the Wolf,
"were never robbed, but you,"
he added, pointing to the Fox,
"have surely stolen something!"

The Cow,
the Goat,
the Sheep
and the Lion

The Cow, the Goat and the Sheep
joined forces with the Lion.
When they had captured a large Stag,
and divided it into shares, the Lion spoke:

"I'll take the first share, because my name is Lion;
you'll give me the second, because I'm strong.
The third will also be mine, because
I'm the most courageous, and whoever
dares touch the fourth will soon regret it."

And so, in his overbearing manner,
he seized the entire prey for himself.

The Fables
of La Fontaine

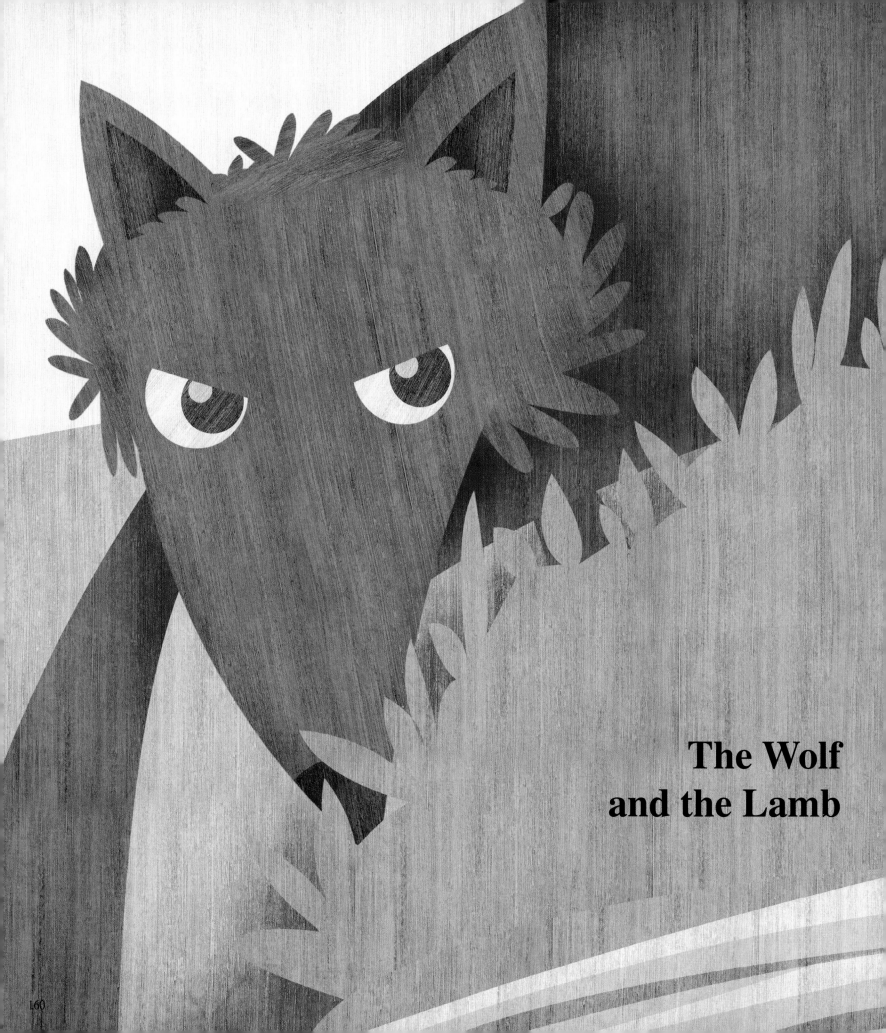

**The Wolf
and the Lamb**

The fable that follows has a hard lesson to learn:
the strongest are always right, no matter where you turn.

One day, a Lamb was drinking, serene,
in the crystal-clear waters of a stream,
when all of a sudden a Wolf appeared
– so hungry he made haste to draw near.
"How dare you muddy my waters?" he furiously cried.

"Master Wolf," the Lamb innocently replied,
"you'll notice, if you just take a look
that I'm drinking much further down the brook,
and so cannot in any way, I think,
have muddied the water that you drink!"
"I stand by my word," the angry Wolf once again cried.
"And last year you spoke ill of me – you cannot lie!"

"A year ago I wasn't even born,
      so it cannot be;
            you're thinking of another lamb,
                  surely not me!"

"Perhaps it was your brother, then,"
said the carnivore.

"I have none, and I'm speaking the truth,
same as before!"

"Nothing but lies!" the Wolf exclaimed.
"One of you is making fun of me;
    I don't like this game."

"I'll soon get my revenge on you all
- sheep, shepherds and dogs, prepare for a fall!"

And so he pounced on him
without a backward glance
… and the poor Lamb
didn't stand a chance.

The Rooster and the Fox

A wise Rooster, keeping watch
from the branches of a tree,
an innocent-looking
Fox chanced to see.

The newcomer exclaimed:
"Peace now reigns
throughout the animal domains.
Can't you see our quarrel's at an end?
Come down so I can embrace you
like a friend!

169

And make haste!," he added, "don't delay
for I must share the news with
several more animals today!
Now you are free to wander and roam;
we'll all be like brothers sharing a home,
happy and joyful, with fireworks in every direction.
Now come down for a kiss that will prove my affection!"

"My friend," the wise Rooster finally replied,
"You've no idea how happy your words make me feel inside.
But you're not the only one I long to embrace;
I see a greyhound running towards us at a furious pace!

He must be a courier sent
to spread the news;
and I'll come down as he joins us,
what say you?"

"I'll leave you to greet him,"
said the Fox in a huff.
"I can't stay – I'm in a rush.
We can celebrate another day."

And so the Fox ran away
through the fields, to join his clan,
angry at the failure of his devious plan.

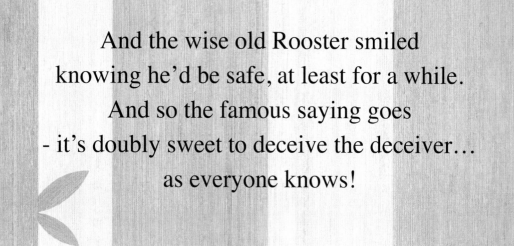

And the wise old Rooster smiled
knowing he'd be safe, at least for a while.
And so the famous saying goes
- it's doubly sweet to deceive the deceiver…
as everyone knows!

The Hen that Laid the Golden Eggs

The following fable has a lesson to teach
those who want too much, and thus overreach.
A Man once had a Hen
who daily laid an egg of gold.

179

And so, believing that a treasure she did hold,
he killed her… only to discover
that inside she was like any other
who laid common eggs, and so he lost
the source of his riches – and oh, at what a cost!
Let this an important lesson be
for those who are never moderate, like me.
People used to tempting fate
are always ready to raise the stakes.
And indeed, they're easy to find
- losing their money, time after time.

The Dove
and the Ant

Drinking from the clear waters of a brook was a Dove,
when all of a sudden an Ant fell in from up above.
She desperately struggled to survive
but wasn't strong enough to beat the tide.

In vain she tried to swim or float
until the compassionate Dove
threw her a "lifeboat"
– a blade of grass,

slender indeed,
but enough for the Ant
to emerge with speed.

A barefoot tramp soon walked by,
armed with a crossbow and a smile most sly.
Upon spying the Dove he decided to shoot…
hoping to take her down with a single shot, to boot!
Aiming his bow, he had only one thought:
a meal fit for a king would soon brew in his pot!

Just then, the clever Ant attacked
his heel with a sharp bite
and, as he looked down,
the Dove took flight.

Into the sky disappeared the dinner
he had so greatly desired,
and so the rascal,
left empty-handed,
retired.

The Fox and the Stork

The Fox one day was so kind
as to invite his friend
the Stork to dine.

The meal was light
and rather meagre;
there was not much to eat,
or to drink either.
All the menu had to offer
was a clear soup,
served on a platter.

And – this should come as no surprise –
the Stork's slender beak kept her
from eating her prize.
But the Fox, ignoring her plight,
ate up all the soup
– not a drop left in sight!

Desiring revenge on the Fox
for his trick,
the Stork returned
the invitation,
quicker than quick.

It was easy enough to convince her sly friend,
who was always hungry, in the end.
The Fox greatly admired the delicious-smelling meal;
chopped into dainty pieces, it was designed to appeal.

But the Stork, with hardened heart
(though it seemed tender),
served the dinner in vases
tall and slender.

The Stork's beak
passed easily
in and out,

an impossible task
for the Fox's
great snout.

And so, dejected and hungry,
the Fox backed away,
its tail between its legs,
as if to say:
"I can't believe
I was tricked by a fowl…
if I had no dignity,
I would let out a howl!"

An important lesson
can hereby be learned:
the trickster must expect
trickery in return.

The Lion Grown Old

The Lion, once the terror
of all the land,
with age his strength
to lose began.

The great beast, once majestic and now pitiful,
was thus attacked by the Horse,
Wolf and Bull.
The unhappy Lion suffered
so much pain
that he thought he would
never roar again.

Resigned to his fate,
he was ready to die,
but when the Donkey showed up,
the Lion sadly cried:

"Oh, I knew my fate was sealed,
but now it's been revealed
that I must face it at your hands...
and it's like dying once again."

The Dog and Its Reflection

All Men cheat themselves, running through life to and fro
in the hopes of touching their own reflection
– though why, no one knows.

They know this story to be true
– the foolish, greedy dog who
seeing his reflection in a brook,
for another dog the image mistook!

Excited about eating a double meal
he dropped his piece of meat,
diving into the water with a squeal.

But there was no other dog,
and instead of eating twice
he nearly drowned,
and lost his own tasty morsel
– if only it had sufficed!

The Frog and the Ox

A Frog no bigger than a chicken egg
saw an enormous Ox, and decided to beg
Nature to grant her the same wondrous size.
So she held her breath and closed her eyes,
and soon began to swell.
"Am I big enough now?" she cried.
"Yes, so please stop
– you'll hurt yourself and your pride!"

But the Frog kept swelling anew
until it burst, and away it flew.

The world is full of such fools
who give themselves airs to change the rules.
How many of these frogs do you know?
Swollen with ambition, there they go!

The Fox and the Sick Lion

One day, the Lion, grown weak and sick
commanded his subjects to visit
– but it was a trick!
He promised them safety
from sharp teeth and jaws
if only they'd keep him
company without pause.

215

While the animals
solemnly marched
into his cave,
the Fox, busy eating,
took care to stay away.

217

And to the other animals he said:
"If you look at the ground,
you'll see tracks coming in,
but none coming back around.
One by one into His Majesty's trap you fall
– let's thank the king for his gift, one and all!
It's a one-way road, can't you see?
So why should I take it?
Explain that to me!"

He who is wicked by nature
can never be trusted.

The Town Mouse
and the Country Mouse

A Country Mouse was invited to town
to dine at his cousin's,
the fanciest house around..

On the Turkish rug was spread a sumptuous feast
– certainly fit for a king rather than a beast!
Though company and food were both divine,
the feast was ruined in no time.

All of a sudden came a loud scratch at the door – a scary noise they had never heard before!

One Mouse escaped leaving
the cake behind,
while the other gave a shriek,
scared out of his mind.
Once the danger had passed,
and the noise had hushed,
the Town Mouse returned

to his seat in a rush,
urging his cousin
to finish the meal.

"No way!" said the other.
"I'm out of here.
Tomorrow come dine with me,
though we won't be feasting
as regally.

But there's no danger
atop a haystack;
we can eat in peace,
without watching our back.
And though in town
your riches are many,
peace is preferable
to fearful plenty."

227

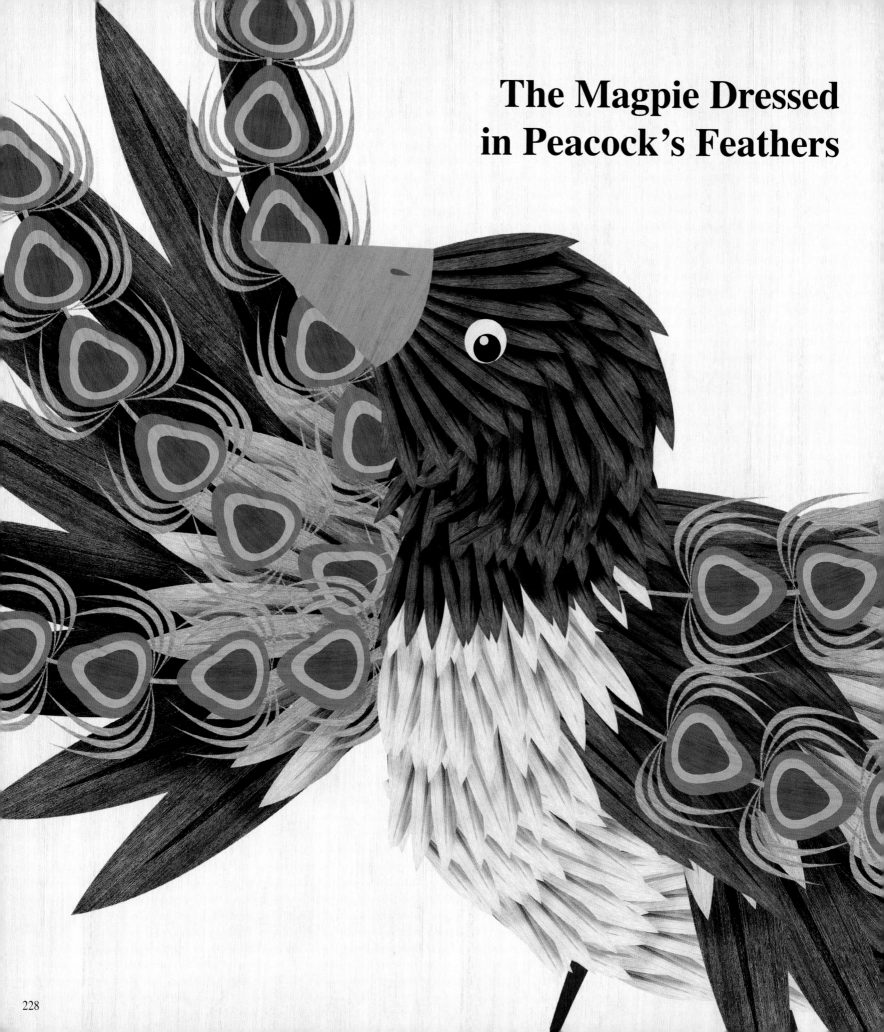

The Magpie Dressed in Peacock's Feathers

It is said that a Magpie found one day
a Peacock's feather's, bright and gay.
Decking himself out in the colorful plumes,
he followed the Peacocks into their room.

They recognized him at once, in spite of his solemn air;
cruelly mocking, even pecking at him,
to his great despair.

So the unlucky Magpie – bitterly hurt –
flew back to his tribe.
But, offended in turn,
they shut him out as he arrived.

Oh, how many two-footed Magpies
with their borrowed plumes love
to parade!

Really, they're just copycats.
And now I've said too much, so…
let's leave it at that.

233

The Fox Who
Had Lost Its Tail

One day, a Fox – the wiliest creature around,
the terror of all the hens and rabbits in town –
got caught in a trap. He managed to break free,
but his lovely tail was not so lucky.

Angry and ashamed,
he hurried home,
where he soon decided
he didn't want to be alone.
So this proposal to
the Fox Council he took,
hoping to convince them
to adopt the new look:

"Are these tails of ours really a must?
We only use them to sweep the roads of dust!
Why not cut them off, just like me –
think how much easier your lives would be!"
"Great idea!," somebody agreed.
"Just turn around, and we shall see!"
And so he did, to general laughter and noise;
thus the long tail remained the fashion of choice.

MARISA VESTITA was born in Taranto in 1975, and begged her parents for private drawing classes ever since she was a little girl. She studied painting at the Lecce Academy of Fine Arts, doing internships in comics, set design and stagecraft at the same time. Driven by her lifelong curiosity for anything concerning the world of images, she moved to Milan in 2002 and began collaborating as an illustrator. A keen interest in the digital world led her to attend a course in Digital Graphics at the Istituto Europeo di Design. To date, she has taken part in several important shows, exhibiting her works all over Italy, as well as collaborating with several Italian publishing companies and magazines. In the past years, she has illustrated several books for White Star Kids, with great enthusiasm and creativity.

WHITE STAR KIDS

White Star Kids® is a registered trademark property of White Star s.r.l.

© 2018 White Star s.r.l.
Piazzale Luigi Cadorna, 6 - 20123 Milan, Italy
www.whitestar.it

Translation and Editing: Contextus, Pavia, Italy
(translator: Daniela Innocenti)

ISBN 978-88-544-1256-9
1 2 3 4 5 6   22 21 20 19 18

Printed in China